KING SMELLY FEET

The illustrations are for
Makiko, with love – J.S

Text copyright © 2002 by Hiawyn Oram. Illustration copyright © 2002 by John Shelley.
This paperback edition first published in 2003 by Andersen Press Ltd. The rights of Hiawyn Oram and John Shelley
to be identified as the author and illustrator of this work have been asserted by them in accordance with the Copyright,
Designs and Patents Act, 1988. First published in Great Britain in 2002 by Andersen Press Ltd. 20 Vauxhall Bridge Road,
London SW1V 2SA. Published in Australia by Random House Australia Pty., 20 Alfred Street, Milsons Point,
Sydney, NSW 2061. Colour separated in Switzerland by Photolitho AG, Zürich.
Printed and bound in Italy by Grafiche AZ, Verona. All rights reserved

10 9 8 7 6 5 4 3 2 1

British Library Cataloguing in Publication Data available.

ISBN 1 84270 243 2

This book has been printed on acid-free paper

KING SMELLY FEET

Written by Hiawyn Oram
and illustrated by John Shelley

A

Andersen Press
London

Once, there were no shoes
and a King who wouldn't wash his feet.

"Ppppooofff!"
said the Queen, holding her nose.

"Pphhewww,"
whispered the Royal Servants.

"Wifferfeet!"
giggled the Children
behind his back.
"Here comes
Stinkitoes!"

One day, the Queen heard
the Children and told the King.
"Oh, very well," he grumbled.
"Just this once, prepare the Royal River
for a Royal Bathe."

So the Royal River was prepared . . .

. . . and the King went in to bathe.
He washed his royal hands, his royal face,
his royal hair, his royal everywhere
and then he washed his royal feet.

"There!" He pulled on his Royal Drying Robe.
"No more Stinkitoes! Here comes King Cleanfeet!"

But as soon as he stepped onto dry land
his clean feet were covered in dust.
"See what I mean?" he bellowed. "Feet-washing is a
waste of royal time. So, either sweep this earth clean –

or I'll be Stinkitoes forever and who cares!"
"I do," thought the Queen.
"We do," muttered the Royal Servants
and the Children's Parents . . .

. . . and they got out their brooms
and swept the land.
But earth being earth, it couldn't be swept.
So the King wouldn't wash his feet,
the Queen and the Royal Servants
could hardly breathe, and the children
giggled behind his back:
"Pong-toes, Pong-soles,
King of all Smelly Feet!"

And the Queen heard and told the King.

"Very well," he grumbled. "If the land won't sweep,
give it a good scrubbing instead and prepare
the Royal River for another Royal Bathe."

So while the Royal Servants
prepared the Royal River . . .

. . . the Queen and the Children's Parents
got out their mops and brushes and scrubbed the land,
and the King went in to bathe.

He washed his royal hands, his royal face,
his royal hair, his royal everywhere . . .
and then he washed his royal feet.

"There!" He pulled on his Royal Drying Robe.
"No more Pong-soles! Just call me Sweet-toes!"

But as soon as he stepped on to dry land
his clean feet were covered in mud.

"See what I mean?" he bellowed.
"Feet-washing is a right waste of royal time.
So either cover this land with something clean or I'll be
King Smelly Feet forever and who cares!"

"I do," thought the Queen.
"We do," thought the Royal Servants and
the Children's Parents . . .

and together they sat down and stitched a giant piece
of clean, strong leather to cover the land.

And the King saw it and bellowed, "That's more like it!
Now, prepare the Royal River for a Right Royal Bathe!"
So the Royal River was prepared . . .

. . . and the King went in to bathe.
He washed his royal hands, his royal face,
his royal hair, his royal everywhere
and then he washed his royal feet.

"There!" He reached for his Royal Drying Robe.
"At last! No more Wifferfeet, Stinkitoes or Pong-soles
because this is going to work!"

But as soon as he stepped onto the clean,
dry leather with his clean feet, the Children gathered round.
"Your Majesty!" they cried. "If the land is covered to keep
your feet clean, the rain won't reach the earth,

the roots won't drink, the grass won't breathe,
the animals won't graze, crops won't grow and we won't eat!"
"Very well!" said the King. "Then bring me some scissors."

So the Royal Servants brought scissors,
which had been invented.

The King cut out two pieces of clean, dry leather
the size of his feet. He cut out two long laces.
With the laces he laced the leather pieces
to the soles of his still clean feet.

"There!" he smiled. "Now *I'm* covered
so the land doesn't have to be.
And, if you don't mind,
I think you'd better call me . . .
King Shoes the First!"